Taken By The Cowboy

Kaci M. Rose

Five Little Roses Publishing

Copyright

Book Cover By: **Cormar Covers**
Editing By: **Violet Rae**

Blurb

A fake date, an ex-fiancé, and a cowboy who's taking what he wants.

Candy

I love my job as the town librarian, but it's pretty hard to meet anyone in a small town like Walker Lake, Texas, and being alone for Christmas sucks.

So, when my friend suggests I be North's fake date to his brother's Christmas wedding, I decide to go for it.

What do I have to lose?

Maybe I should have gotten all the details first...

North

My brother is marrying my ex-fiancée, and my parents want me to go and put on a brave face for the sake of the family.

I will do it for them, but I refuse to go alone. So, when a buddy of mine suggests taking the curvy librarian as my fake date, I am all in.

Candy is as sweet as her name, and I have no intention of letting her walk away—but my ex has other plans.

With the whole town watching my every move, I plan on taking what I want.

And what I want is Candy...

Contents

Get Free Books!

Would you like some free cowboy books?
**If you join Kaci M. Rose's Newsletter you get
books and bonus epilogues free!**

**Join Kaci M. Rose's newsletter and get your
free books!**
https://www.kacirose.com/KMR-Newsletter

Now on to the story!

Chapter 1

North

"I don't know why the fuck you're going to this wedding," my best friend, Ben, says as we sit at the diner for lunch.

How many times have I asked myself the same question? I sure as hell don't want to be at my brother's Christmas wedding. Why? Because he's marrying my ex.

Finding out Vikki was cheating on me with Jake was bad enough, but now my parents are insisting I go to their wedding as if nothing has happened.

"I'm going because my grandparents, who I haven't seen in two years, will be there. With my grandfather's health, this might be the last time they can make the trip, and I'd never forgive myself if I didn't see them. But I'm sure as hell not going alone."

I hope Ben has an idea of who I can ask. He's a cop and seems to know everyone in the small town of Walker Lake, Texas. He's in full uniform, and it doesn't go unnoticed by the locals—especially the single ladies. Not that he has eyes for any of them. He's keeping his head down and working toward getting his own ranch.

He looks around the small diner where we're having lunch—the only decent place in town to grab a bite. "Why don't you ask Candy? She's the town librarian."

He nods to a corner of the diner behind me, where a woman sits, eating lunch alone and reading a book. She's gorgeous, curvy, and looks sweet enough to eat. Dark brown hair flows in waves over her shoulders. Is she as sweet as her name suggests? Whatever she's reading in that book has a smile on her face.

"You think she'd go for it?" I ask.

Ben shrugs. "Only one way to find out."

He's right. I stand and take a deep breath before walking over to her table. She's so wrapped up in her book that she doesn't notice me, so I sit in the seat across from her.

Only then does she look up at me, putting the book down and offering me a sweet smile. "Oh, you're Ben's friend. Your name is North, right?"

I don't know why I take pride in the fact she knows who I am, but I do.

It's a small town, and everyone knows Ben. Hell, everyone knows everyone. I generally keep my head down, but even I know most people in the diner.

"Yes, and you're Candy, the librarian."

She nods and offers me a small smile.

I look back at Ben to see he's watching our exchange. "Okay, so long story short, my brother is marrying my ex, and my parents are insisting I go to the wedding, plus I want to see my grandparents who will be there. It's a weeklong event here in town, mostly in the evenings. And we'll also be taking part in some of the town Christmas events. I don't want to go to this wedding alone. Would you be willing to go with me? I'll pay for everything, and I'll even pay for your time." I know I'm rambling as I rush to get all the details out.

I almost expect Candy to laugh, thinking it's a joke, but she doesn't. She looks at me like she's seriously considering my offer, but she doesn't say anything.

"What do you think?" I'm desperate to know what's going on in that beautiful head.

"Well, I could use the money with my sister in school."

That wasn't a no, so I push my luck a little more. "Maybe we can pretend we've been dating for a little while?"

Candy purses her lips. She thinks for a minute and then looks over at Ben. I don't dare take my eyes off her to turn around and see what his reaction is.

Then she looks over at Austin, who runs the diner. She's back behind the counter, and I'm pretty sure the two of them are friends.

Candy smiles. "Okay, but I'm a writer, so I make no promises that I won't write this into a book."

I let out a breath and realizing that there's nothing I wouldn't do to get her to agree hits me hard. "Deal. Can I take you to dinner tomorrow so we can get our story straight?"

"That's probably a good idea. Let me give you my number."

We exchange phone numbers and make plans for tomorrow. I couldn't have asked for a better fake date. She's sweet and gorgeous and everything my ex wasn't.

Having to go to this wedding suddenly doesn't seem so bad.

Chapter 2

Candy

We agreed to meet at the park on the lake, but I didn't expect North to cook dinner. I thought maybe he'd grab something from the diner, but he set out a blanket on the ground for a picnic by the lake.

"So, tell me about yourself," I say as I bite into a piece of the fried chicken he's made.

"It's me, my mom and dad, and Jake, who's marrying my ex. My grandparents don't live in town, but they'll be here for the wedding. It's possibly the last time they'll be able to make this trip here."

North has a wistful look as he talks about his grandparents. It's easy to see how much he loves them.

"So, your ex cheated on you with your brother?" I'm eager to know the whole story because I'm sure it'll be expected if his family thinks we've been dating for a while.

"Yes. I was about to propose when I discovered Vikki was cheating on me with Jake. I stopped going to family events if they were there. My parents acted like nothing was wrong, and I think it's because they didn't know how to handle it. They didn't want to lose their son, but they pushed me away in the process."

I can tell this is a difficult topic for him, so I change the subject. "What do you do for a living, North?"

He offers me a grateful smile like he's thankful for the change of subject. "I worked on the oil rigs for a while, saved a bunch of money, and bought a ranch here in town. It's small compared to some, but plenty big to keep me well entertained. What about you? What's your story?"

I take a moment to think about what would be important for him to know, especially if we were dating for real. "I was raised by my dad, the most amazing man in the world, and I have a little sister in school. I started working as soon as possible to help my dad out and studied hard to get my master's degree in the amount of time it takes most people to get their bachelor's. I worked my way through school, and every extra penny I have helps put my sister through school."

We talk a bit more before North walks me back to my house behind the downtown library.

"I'd like to take you out a few more times to get to know you better, so I'm not truly lying to my mom," North says as he drops me off at my place.

I agree and then head inside.

· · · ● ● · ● · · ·

The following day on my lunch break, I head to the diner to see my friend, Austin, who runs the place. She's talking to her sister, Natalie, which is perfect because I could use their opinions.

Austin puts in our food order, and we grab a table while I spill the details of helping out North.

"I think you need to be careful and remember this isn't real. You're not dating for real," Austin advises.

Natalie agrees, and I know they're right. I'm the chubby friend helping him out, and I'm okay with that.

We talk about Natalie's son, Nate, and how her husband is doing. She glows when she talks about her husband and son. Having that kind of love is something I hope to find someday.

As we finish up, North walks in.

"Ladies," he greets us with a tilt of his hat.

Austin and Natalie make their excuses, leaving us alone with winks and knowing smiles.

"I didn't mean to chase your friends off." North smiles and takes a seat across from me.

"We were finishing up lunch. It's okay."

"So, you've already eaten. Can I convince you to stick around while I have lunch?" he asks with a flirty grin.

I remind myself this isn't real. He's putting on a show for the town in case it gets back to his parents.

"I could go for a milkshake, but I can't stay too long."

That seems to make him happy, and he places our order. We talk easily about siblings and parents and what he does on the ranch. I share what an average workday looks like for me, and we talk about all the basic stuff we need to know each other, trying to cover all the bases.

After lunch, North walks me back to the library, and I give him a quick tour until a group of people walks in.

He gives me a quick kiss on the cheek, tips his hat, and leaves.

Too bad none of this is real. It would be the best relationship of my life so far.

Chapter 3

North

I invite Candy to my ranch for our third date and show her around. I figure if we'd been dating a while, she would have seen it.

Once I'm done giving her a tour of the barn and the horses, I invite her inside for lunch. The horses love her, as do the barn cats, and she seems to fit right in. I remind myself that this isn't real. She's not here to stay, and it doesn't matter if she fits in because she's not staying.

"So, I was thinking with this timeline, we need to spend some time with my family too," Candy says.

"Of course." It's the holidays, and a real couple would split time between both families.

"What does the wedding timeline look like?" she asks.

"Well, it starts this weekend with the Christmas festival downtown. Then over the next week, it's a few different dinners. The Christmas light cruise, the bachelor and bachelorette parties, the rehearsal dinner the night before, and the wedding at a lake house on Christmas Eve."

"We should have dinner with my dad before then, and he'll want me for Christmas dinner if I'm going to miss Christmas Eve."

That's fair, and after spending the entire week with my family and the stress of all this, I'm not going to want to see them for Christmas.

Candy bites her lip, lost in thought, and it's driving me crazy. What I wouldn't give to taste those lips right now.

A crazy idea pops into my head. It'll be kind of obvious if we haven't kissed. "You know, maybe we should get the awkward first kiss out of the way. We want to look comfortable with each other in front of my family."

Candy looks down at her lap, and her face turns bright red. It's sexy as hell, but when she looks up at me, I see the determination in her eyes.

"Okay."

• • • ● • ● • ● • •

Candy

Holy hell, I've agreed to kiss North. The sexy cowboy who wears his Wranglers just right, has muscles for days, tattoos down his arms, and smells like you'd expect a cowboy to smell—all fresh air, leather, and woodsy goodness.

He could get any girl, yet he wants a fake relationship and a real kiss with me. And he's right—we can't have that awkward first kiss in front of anyone. It would blow out the whole cover.

Although I wasn't prepared at all for this. Our kiss has to look authentic while keeping North at a distance because this isn't a real relationship.

Maybe Austin is right, and I haven't thought this all the way through. It won't be as easy as I thought, but I gave him my word, so I'm going to follow through. What his brother did to him was bull hockey, and I don't want him to have to do it alone.

North steps closer and rests his hand on my waist. His eyes lock on mine, holding me in place. He cups my cheek before slowly leaning toward me, and it feels like forever before his lips gently brush mine.

The sensation of his lips on mine causes me to gasp. His grip on my waist tightens, and he lets out the softest moan before pulling me in and deepening the kiss.

Every nerve in my body reacts to his proximity, and I melt into him. I was determined to keep my walls up, but I'm lost in one of the best kisses of my damn life. It isn't rushed or awkward. It's soft, slow, and panty-melting.

We're both breathing heavily when he finally pulls away. The heat in his eyes makes me want to kiss him again, but this wasn't a kiss for fun. This was so we didn't blow our cover.

I head home, dazed from that kiss. How is it possible the first time I've been truly kissed was for a fake relationship? And even though I know it's fake, I'm already hoping to do it again.

Since I'm having dinner with my dad tonight, I head straight there. My sister gets into town tomorrow for her school break, so I know he'll want to make plans, and I need to ensure he knows about North.

"You're early." Dad wraps me in a tight hug, greeting me as if he hasn't seen me in years when we had dinner together only last week.

"Hey, Dad. I wanted to talk before we had dinner. I know you're trying to make plans for when Parker gets home."

"What's wrong? Is everything okay? What do you need?" He immediately goes into protective dad mode, and I love that about him.

"Nothing is wrong. I'm seeing someone, and his brother is getting married over Christmas, so there are a few events I need to attend with him."

Dad breaks out into a huge smile. "Let's go inside, and you can tell me all about him. I'm glad you're finally dating."

Dad's been worried that I haven't been dating, which makes me feel guilty about this all being fake with North.

Chapter 4

North

C andy called last night and said her dad wanted to meet me. Since her sister's in town, they're going to pick a Christmas tree and asked if I wanted to go. Of course, I want to go, even though I shouldn't. This dating thing with Candy should only be for appearances. But I haven't been to a Christmas tree farm since I was a little boy, and I can't resist the temptation of spending time with Candy.

To say I'm nervous as I drive to her dad's house would be an understatement. I know how important her dad is to her, and I don't want to screw it up for her. She's doing me a huge favor, and she can't be happy lying to her dad about us, which makes me feel even worse about the fake date thing.

When I pull up to the address Candy gave me, she's sitting on the front porch steps and comes to meet me before I even get out of my truck.

"Everything okay?" I ask, worried that something's changed.

"I wanted to say thank you for this. I know it wasn't part of the deal."

"Of course it was. I agreed to a few family events for you too. It's only fair. I wouldn't expect you to miss out on spending time with your family for me. After you get done hanging out with my family, you'll understand," I say wryly.

I take her hand as we head toward the house. An older man, who I assume is her father, and a younger girl who looks like Candy meet us out on the porch.

"North, this is my dad, Bill, and my sister, Parker. Guys, this is North."

When we talked last night, Candy said this would be a good test. Her dad is inquisitive, so if we can pass his scrutiny without raising any suspicions, we should be good to go with my family.

As we head to Bill's truck, I open the passenger door for Parker before climbing into the back seat with Candy. I hold her hand the whole way and answer any questions her dad throws my way.

I soon realize that picking out Christmas trees means Candy and Parker do the picking while her dad and I stand back and give our opinion whenever we're asked.

"So, how did you two meet?" Bill asks as the girls bounce from tree to tree.

Candy and I talked about this and decided to stay as close to the truth as possible. Neither one of us likes lying to our family.

"My friend, Ben, introduced us."

"Ben the cop?"

"Yep. We've been friends since high school."

"He's a good guy. He just bought a ranch not far from here. A small hobby ranch."

Anything under a hundred acres is considered a hobby ranch around here, even though it's big enough to support a family if done right.

Bill tells the girls to choose a bigger tree than the one they've picked out, which makes them light up. "Candy said your brother is getting married next week?"

"Yeah, and I know you guys have a lot of family plans, but I'm grateful she's going with me. My brother is marrying my ex. She cheated on me while we were dating," I tell him honestly.

Bill looks shocked. "Christ, why are you even going?"

I frown as I consider his question. "Because my parents said it's family, and apparently, that means I have to be there." I shrug, trying to brush it off.

He looks at me from the corner of his eye, and I know he wants to say something.

"What is it?" I finally ask, wanting to know what he's thinking.

"I love my girls, but I wouldn't support one betraying the other like that. Have you told your parents you don't want to go?"

"Oh, yes. But it doesn't matter. My mom used every ounce of mom guilt she had on me and convinced my grandparents to come to the wedding. They haven't been able to visit for a few years, so she knew I wouldn't miss the chance to see them."

"It might not be my place, but you should be protecting yourself, not putting yourself in a situation like this."

Bill is brutally honest, but he's only saying what I've been thinking. I'd never do this to one of my kids.

Thankfully, we move on to lighter topics, and after our conversation, Bill seems more accepting of having me in his daughter's life.

Once we get the tree back to Bill's place, the girls immediately pull out the boxes to start decorating.

The time with Candy's family flies by as we decorate the Christmas tree and have lunch before I help Bill decorate outside. It's a reminder of how my family used to be before Jake and Vikki did the dirty on me. We were close—the kind of close where nothing could break the bond—or so I thought. Turns out that bond wasn't so strong after all.

Candy has a permanent smile on her face when I drive her home later that night. My emotions are entering dangerous territory with her, but all I can think about is how I can keep that smile on her face.

Chapter 5

Candy

We arrive at the Christmas festival the following day, where I'm meeting North's family. Was North this nervous about meeting my dad? If he was, he sure as hell didn't show it.

We barely get inside the main festival area before we're waylaid by people he knows. I refuse to leave North's side. Having him close calms me, especially when he holds my hand in his warm one and rubs his thumbs over my knuckles.

"I promise you'll be fine," he whispers in my ear as we finish talking to one of his friends.

But the further we walk into the festival, the more nervous he gets.

"Calm down. I'm here to support you," I reassure him.

He wraps his arm around my waist and leans into me. "This is the first time I've seen my ex since we broke up. I've avoided family functions when I knew they'd be there.

That's when I notice a blonde in a blue dress walking our way.

She sees North, and her face lights up as she stops in front of us. "North, sweetheart. I'm so happy you're here."

She smiles and places her hand on his arm. North stiffens, and his grip tightens around my waist.

The blonde's eyes flick over me as she sizes me up. "Who's this?" she asks as a man walks up beside her and places his hand on the small of her back.

"This is my girlfriend, Candy. Candy, this is my brother, Jake, and his fiancée, Vikki." North introduces us.

"Candy. Isn't that a stripper's name?" Vikki asks with a smirk.

"Candy as in candy cane. My mother craved them while she was pregnant with me, so now, I'm paying for it." I offer her a genuine smile and try to keep things civil.

"She's not your type. This has to be a joke," Vikki says, dropping her fake smile.

"She's not you, which is exactly my type," North snaps.

He pulls me away without another word and leads me to the other side of the room. "I'm so sorry about her," he apologizes, searching my face to gauge my reaction.

"It's okay." I shrug and offer him a smile.

"No, it's not," he says, and before I can reply, he leans down and kisses me.

I'm not sure if he's putting on a show, but I go along with it, wrapping my arms around his neck and pulling him in closer.

A throat clears beside us, and North pulls back. I look over to see an older man and woman standing beside us.

"Mom. Dad," North greets them, tugging me against his side.

"Who's this beautiful girl?" His mom smiles at me.

"Mom, this is my girlfriend, Candy. Candy, this is my mom, Janette, and my dad, Tom."

"It's nice to meet you. Who are your parents?" Janette asks.

This is a typical question around here. If they don't recognize you, they ask about your parents to try to pinpoint who you are.

"Bill Ellenson," I tell her.

"Oh, Bill is such a great guy," Tom says. "He helped when I got sick and took over the BBQ festival a couple of years back."

Janette nods in recognition. "Oh, you must invite him to the wedding."

North tenses beside me. I know that's not part of the plan.

"I'm sure he'd love to, but my little sister is home from college, and they're spending time together. She told me she's excited to have Dad to herself this week. I don't dare ruin that for her because they don't get much time together."

"Please make sure you say hi for us. And let him know we've been thinking about him," Janette says right before they get pulled away.

North blows out a breath and turns to me with a smile. "You've earned some fun time at the festival. Come on."

He pulls me farther into the crowd, and we stroll around, looking at local craft vendors and tasting the different foods. Then we head for the Ferris wheel, where we run into Sarah and Mac.

Sarah used to work at the dinner before Mac made his move after years of being her friend. She now lives down in Rock Springs, Texas, with his family.

"They'll expect us to kiss at the top, and everyone will be watching," North whispers as we are seated in our car on the Ferris wheel.

It's true. Couples are expected to kiss at the top, and I'm sure his family is watching. I've felt eyes on me all night.

My nerves ramp up as we start the slow climb to the top. North takes my hand and tries to calm me. When he leans in and his lips finally land on mine for the second time today, it still feels like the first time. I don't know what to think of it. I expected the novelty of kissing him to have worn off by now.

If it feels like the first time every time he kisses me, I won't make it through the week.

Chapter 6

North

I'm so dumbstruck by our kiss at the top of the Ferris wheel that I consider begging her to go around again. But I know that that would be pushing things. I can't seem to get enough of her, and that's dangerous territory considering this situation has an end date.

As we step off the Ferris wheel, I see Ben waiting in line, a knowing smirk on his face.

"Candy, is he treating you well?" he asks.

She smiles. "Yeah, he is."

"But my ex isn't treating her so well," I tell him.

"I never liked her." He sighs and then looks at Candy again. "You can always send me an SOS text if you need to get out of there."

"Thanks." She smiles and looks up at me.

I don't like the idea of her needing an out to get away from me or my ex, but I know she'll feel more comfortable if she has one. I reach for her hand, and we step back into the festival.

We notice Vikki off to the side, glaring at us. Jake is with her and looks pissed off that she's staring at us. I can only imagine their conversation—probably about why she cares who I'm here with. It's okay for her to move on, but not me.

"I guess we won't be friends anytime soon." Candy shrugs and brushes it off.

We head toward a few more rides, and I block out everything except Candy. It's just the two of us, and we don't need anyone interfering with what should be a fun time. She's doing me a huge favor, and I want her to enjoy herself and not feel like she has to constantly play a part.

As we're getting ready to leave, I get a text from my mom saying she'd like to have Candy and me over for dinner tomorrow to get to know her. No other details, like if Jake and Vikki will be there.

"My mom wants to have dinner with us tomorrow so she can get to know you better," I tell her as we walk back to my car.

"Oh, that's fine. Just let me know when. The library closes at four thirty tomorrow."

"There's a good chance my brother and ex will be there."

"That's fine. Tell me how you want me to handle it." Candy shrugs like it's no big deal.

"What do you mean, how I want you to handle it?"

"I can be the polite girlfriend, or we can completely ignore them. We can be the PDA couple who flirt and hug and kiss, or we can be slightly vindictive, and every time Vikki looks at you, I'll remind her that you're mine now."

I grin. She may be sweet as candy, but she's got a bit of an evil streak in her, and I fucking love it.

I have every intention of replying that she should be the polite girlfriend and we'll get out of there as quickly as possible, but that's not what comes out of my mouth. "Is there a mix of the PDA couple and a slightly vindictive new girlfriend?"

She smiles. "That can be arranged."

I walk her to the door when we get to her little cabin behind the library. Maybe it's a fake relationship, but I'm still a gentleman. "I'll pick you up tomorrow at five."

Without thinking, I lean in and place a soft kiss on her lips. She melts into me like I was hoping she would. Her soft curves feel amazing against me, and I know we're entering dangerous territory.

• • • ● • • ● ● • • •

Thankfully, Jake and Vikki aren't at dinner, and Candy visibly relaxes when she realizes. I don't blame her one bit.

She's in the kitchen helping my mom while I sit in the living room with my dad.

"How long have you two been seeing each other?" Dad asks once the women have disappeared into the other room.

"Not very long. I wasn't going to invite her to all the wedding stuff, but when she found out about Jake and Vikki, she said she didn't want me to go through it alone, so here we are." I shake my head. "Vikki's already made it known that Candy isn't my type, and her jealous side is coming out, so this wedding will be . . . interesting."

My dad never liked Vikki when I was dating her, and he still doesn't, but he loves my mom and will do anything to keep the peace. My mom seems to think this is the best way to do that. If she only knew how wrong she was.

"Your mom's having a Christmas dinner before your brother and Vikki leave for their honeymoon," Dad says.

I know what he's getting at. He wants me to come to Christmas dinner even though I've made it clear I won't attend any events if Jake and Vikki are there.

"I won't be there." I hold up a hand as Dad starts to protest. "Candy's giving up a lot of her time to be with me for this wedding. Her sister's in town from school, and she won't get to spend as much time with her, so we're doing Christmas dinner with her dad and her sister. I owe her that."

My dad pauses for a minute but then nods because he gets it.

I smirk. "I'm sure they'd be happy to set another plate if you need to get away."

He laughs. "Don't tell me."

Over dinner, Mom talks about the Christmas light cruise out on the lake tomorrow. I can't think of anything worse than being trapped on a boat with Jake and Vikki, but it's one of the required events, and my grandmother has been looking forward to it.

"So, the wedding will be at this cabin a bit farther up the lake," Mom says, pausing to take a sip of her drink. "Since North will be staying the night before the wedding, we'd also like to have you come. I wouldn't normally approve of unmarried couples sharing a room, but I think I could look the other way this time."

Candy's cheeks color the most beautiful shade of pink.

"That's up to Candy. This whole thing is awkward and uncomfortable for everyone, so I'm not going to force her," I tell my mom, also letting Candy know she has an out.

She places her hand on my thigh under the table and smiles. "It's fine. I'll be there, but I'll drive my car just in case."

She gives me a flirty wink that doesn't go unnoticed by my mom.

After dinner, Candy and my mom do the dishes. I love that despite everything, they get along so well. Under different circumstances, it could make me hope for something more. Even if Candy and I were dating for real, there would never be anything more then this with my parents. There are no big family events in my future in fact there's probably more fighting than anything else.

On the way home, all I can think about is sharing a room with Candy, and the thought alone is making me hard as hell.

"You don't have to spend the night at the cabin," I tell her. I'm trying to give her yet another out.

"I'd like to be there for you. I'm sure it's not going to be easy, and if nothing else, we're friends, right?"

"Candy, I don't want to be just your friend," I tell her as I reach her front door.

I lean in and place another kiss on her lips. This kiss is for us because I've quickly become addicted to her.

I force myself to pull away, and the dazed look on her face is sexy as fuck. When she looks at me, I know what I feel for her is much more than friendship.

"Would you like to come inside?" she whispers.

There's nothing I want more. I nod because I don't think I can find my voice.

She opens the door, and I follow her inside. I watch her every move as she steps out of her heels and places her purse and jacket on the table. I remove my shoes and jacket before following her to the couch.

She looks down at her lap, where her hands fiddle nervously. When she speaks, her voice is so soft I almost miss it. "I don't think I want to be just your friend, either."

My heart stops. Her expression is uncertain when she looks up at me. So, I do the only thing I can to reassure her.

I kiss her again. And again. And again.

I never want to take my lips from hers. I pull her into my lap and try to ignore how hard my cock is, how badly I want to run my hands over every inch of her, and how much I want to kiss every one of her curves.

I don't know how long we kiss—days, hours, or a few minutes—but when we pull apart, we're both breathing heavily. Goosebumps cover her arms, her lips are swollen, and her cheeks have a beautiful flush.

I kiss her forehead. "Get some sleep, Candy Cane. We have a long night tomorrow."

She stands and walks me to the door.

The last thing I want to do is leave her, but the last thing I can do is stay.

Chapter 7

Candy

How the hell am I so attracted to this guy? I've talked to him here and there around town, but we've never gotten to know each other until now. But after that little make-out session on my couch, I can't sleep to save my life. I kept thinking about him and what I wanted him to do to me instead of getting up and leaving.

There's no way he feels the same. Hot guys like him don't go for the curvy nerdy librarians like me.

As I'm getting ready for work the following morning, Austin calls.

She doesn't even say hello. "Girl, everyone is talking about that kiss at the top of the Ferris wheel, and I need the details. What's going on?"

"His whole family was watching and expecting a kiss at the top. When we got down, pretty much everyone had seen it, including his ex, who was shooting daggers at me for the rest of the night."

"Why didn't I hear from you yesterday? I was expecting a girl's night with details."

"His mom invited us to dinner. She wanted to get to know me better. Thankfully, North's brother and ex weren't there, and his mom's lovely when she's not around them. After dinner, North brought me home, and..." I trail off, unsure if I want to share that part with her.

But Austin's always been good at reading me and knows when there's more to the story. "And?" she asks gently, pushing me along.

"And we had a bit of a make-out session on my couch before he left."

Neither of us says anything for a moment.

"I can tell by your tone that your heart is already involved, isn't it?" Her soft tone reminds me of the one I use on my little sister when giving her advice she doesn't want to hear.

"I didn't plan on the kissing and how it would make me feel."

"There's a good chance that sleeping with him could get him out of your system. Or it could make you feel even more for him."

"So, I'm damned if I do and damned if I don't?"

"Pretty much," she says unhelpfully. "Listen, have fun tonight and try to get a read on him. If he's standoffish, then you know things went a bit too far. Follow his lead and go with your gut. Relationships have started over a lot less."

"Austin, this isn't some romance book. Guys like him don't fall for fat girls like me."

"I'm coming to the library at lunch to whoop your ass for calling yourself fat. I don't know who put it into your head that it's okay to talk to yourself like that. You're fucking gorgeous, and the right man will love your curves because I would kill for them."

We've had conversations like this many times. I try to love my body, but I wasn't always over-weight. I was skinny in school and then busted my butt in college to get my degrees early. The stress made gaining weight easier than losing it, and my college boyfriend made it very clear how he felt about that.

I guess it's easy to believe the bad things but a lot harder to believe the good things, no matter how hard your best friend tries to reassure you.

My nerves are in full flight by the time North knocks on my door. I'm in jeans and a dressy sweater since I know it will be colder out on the water. When I open the door, I'm not expecting him to eat me up with his eyes. He looks at me like I'm wearing the sexiest lingerie he's ever seen.

"I can go change..." I start to say.

"Don't you dare. You look stunning." He steps forward, places a hand on my hip, and kisses my cheek.

He keeps his hand on my lower back as he guides me to the car and opens my car door like a gentleman. Starting the car, he reaches over and holds my hand the whole way, asking about my day and telling me about his.

"My dad wants to know if you can come over for breakfast tomorrow," I ask him shyly, remembering my conversation with Dad at lunch. "My sister has something planned, so it would just be the three of us,"

Dad seems to be under the impression that things are a bit more serious between us than they are. I'm not sure how he thinks that, considering this is all fake.

"Sure. And since we have an off day tomorrow with no wedding events, why don't we go out and do something, just you and me?"

I want to ask if he means an actual date, but then I remember that people in town expect to see us out together, especially on a night when we don't have any wedding events.

I agree, and we head on to the boat for the wedding party Christmas light cruise. We say our hellos, but the bride and groom avoid us, which is fine with me, and by the looks of it, with North too.

As the boat leaves the dock and starts heading around the lake, I find a spot leaning against one of the handrails and take in the view. North joins me, pressing his front to my back and resting his hands on either side of mine on the rail. He rests his head beside mine as we relax and watch the lights, ignoring everyone else around us.

"You look beautiful in this light," he whispers, and my cheeks heat with a blush. "And you look sexy as hell when you blush like that too. I didn't sleep a wink last night because you had me so damn turned on, baby."

He runs his nose down my neck. He's teasing me, but I can feel how hard he is, so he's teasing himself as much as me.

His soft caresses and teasing continue for the rest of the cruise, and by the time we head home, I'm so damn turned on I think I might explode if he doesn't touch me.

Chapter 8

North

I had no idea something as simple as a cruise around the lake to look at Christmas lights could be such a damn turn-on. But having Candy pressed against me the whole time was equal amounts of torture and pleasure. And she knew exactly what she was doing when she wiggled against me. I was hard all night, but on the flip side, I got to hold her in my arms. This has become so much more than a simple fake relationship for my brother's wedding. I never expected to feel like this for her.

It's easy to convince myself this is a real relationship because it feels like one. It's what I desperately want, but I have no idea if Candy feels the same way. I'm hoping the way she kisses me means she does.

We get to her house, and I walk her to the door, her hand in mine. When we reach the door, she stops and looks back at me, and I see the desire in her eyes. Tonight turned her on as much as me.

"Would you like to come in?" she asks.

I hesitate for a moment. I should turn around and head home. I should politely turn her down because if I go in, I won't be able to stop after all the teasing tonight. But I also know I can't walk away from her. What we have has a deadline unless I can figure out a way to convince her that we're more.

"Yeah, I would," I tell her, stepping inside as she opens the door.

"Would you like some hot chocolate? I think it'd be a great way to warm up after being out on the lake all night," she says as she makes her way toward the kitchen.

I get the feeling she needs to be busy because she's nervous. "Hot chocolate sounds great." I follow her to the kitchen and sit at the small table, watching her move around the kitchen, opening cupboards and starting some hot chocolate on the stove.

"Do you like marshmallows in your hot chocolate? I don't have any whipped cream, but I have a ton of marshmallows," she rambles nervously.

"Marshmallows are perfect."

Candy busies herself making the hot chocolate. She finally brings two mugs over and sets them down on the table. I pull the other chair closer so when she sits down, our legs are touching. I lean forward and place my hand on her knee as we drink our hot chocolate. Her eyes stay on my hand, and she doesn't look at me.

"This doesn't feel much like a fake relationship anymore," she whispers with her eyes still on my hand.

"No, it doesn't," I agree, inching my hand up her leg.

Candy finally looks at me, and I know I need to take my chance. "What if it wasn't fake? What if you were mine?"

A look of hope sparks in her eyes, and she nods. I know this is a conversation we need to have, but I want her more than my next breath.

Slowly, I reach for her shirt, and when she doesn't stop me, I remove it and let it fall to the floor. I trace the line of her bra, and her breathing picks up. "Are you sure you want this, sweetheart?" My voice is rough because the idea of stopping kills me.

"Yes," she whispers.

That's all I need. I make quick work of the rest of her clothes and stand to admire her naked curves while removing my clothes. The ideas that run through my head have me beyond excited.

"Stand up for me, beautiful." I hold my hand out to her, and she does as I ask.

I let my eyes roam over every inch of her skin. She's so damn sexy. I grab her around the waist and set her on the table. She lets out a little squeal of surprise, making her tits jiggle and my dick throb.

I fall to my knees in front of her and spread her legs wide. She tries to fight me and keep them closed, but a soft kiss on the inside of each thigh has her relaxing and letting me in.

When her pussy is on full display for me, I run a finger from her clit to her slit, and her whole body shudders. She's wet for me, and it's such a damn turn-on.

I grab her hips and pull her ass to the edge of the table. "Lie back, baby."

Candy does as I ask, and I lean in to get my first taste of her. She tastes as sweet as her name. She grips my hair, and I show no mercy, flicking her clit with my tongue and drinking down every drop. She moans my name, which only spurs me on. Fuck, the sound alone is almost enough to make me come right then and there.

I reach down and squeeze my cock almost to the point of pain because every drop is going inside her. I don't want to waste a single bit. Thankfully, she comes on my tongue a moment later, and I keep her orgasm going until she's lying on the table purring.

I stand up and step between her legs, sliding my hand over her soft stomach to pinch her nipples. "Don't move, baby. I need to go grab a condom."

Before I can move, she grabs my wrist. "I'm on the pill and it's been a long time since I've been with anyone."

"I was tested after I found out Vikki was cheating. I'd love to have you raw, but that's a huge step, babe." I tell her, trying to dampen my excitement.

"I know, but it feels right with you."

Fuck, yeah, it does because I plan to make this girl mine. Not just tonight, but for good.

I pull her legs around my waist and line up my cock to her entrance. We lock eyes as I slide into her for the first time, and we both moan. I've never been bareback before, but fuck, her went warm walls hugging my cock is heaven.

Goosebumps race across her skin, and she arches her back to take even more of me, which pushes her hard nipples in the air. I can't stop myself from leaning down and tasting them.

I angle my hips as I start thrusting because I need her to come again. I crave it more than my next breath, but I also know I won't last long. She feels too good and looks too fucking sexy lying here taking my cock.

"You've got to come, baby. Soak my cock because you feel so good."

"Don't... oh... stop... no... harder..." She can't form a complete sentence, and it's the best compliment.

I give her what she wants, and I lose it as she starts to come. I come so hard that my vision blurs. The tighter she clamps down on me, the more intense my climax becomes before I finally collapse on top of her.

Fuck, I'm going to marry this girl.

· · · ● · ● · · ·

We ended up in bed at some point last night, and I wake up the next morning with her in my arms. There's no better feeling in the world than knowing your girl is in your arms after a great night of sex.

As Candy stirs, I hold her tighter until she wraps her arms around me.

"Good morning," she mumbles in her sleepy voice, and it's so damn sexy.

"Good morning, beautiful. How did you sleep?" I ask as I lazily run a hand up and down her back.

"Better than I have in a long time."

"Me too. Why don't you pack a bag and stay at my place tonight?" I ask because there's nothing I'd love more than to have her in my bed.

"Okay."

"Why don't you get ready? I'll head home to shower and change, and then I'll come back and pick you up so we can go and hang out with your dad."

Candy nods, and we get moving, even though we're both reluctant to get out of bed.

Chapter 9

Candy

I have a fantastic time with North, my dad, and my sister. He fits right in like the missing puzzle piece in our family. When we sit down for brunch, he's constantly touching me, whether it's his arm across the back of my chair while he rubs my shoulder or placing his warm hand on my thigh.

It's enough to drive me crazy. Thankfully my dad has mercy on us and kicks us out the door to enjoy some time together before the bachelor and bachelorette parties.

We decide to drive the hour into Amarillo and play tourist. We visit the Cadillac ranch in the RV museum before having dinner and heading back to North's place. It was nice to get out of town and not have to answer endless questions about our relationship.

But walking into North's house this time, my nerves hit full force. It's not like the last time

I was here, and we were under the whole fake relationship guise. This time it's just us.

"You know a chaise lounge seems wildly out of place for a cowboy ranch," I comment on the piece of furniture in his living room.

"That's what happens when you ask your mom to help you decorate. She loves that thing. She'd never forgive me if she came over and it wasn't here because she always sits there, so I'm stuck with it."

I slowly walk over to it and sit down, draping myself over it before looking at him. "I guess I can see the appeal. It's pretty comfortable and relaxing."

Pure heat sparks in his eyes as he slowly walks over and sits beside me. He trails a finger along my neck, between my breasts, and down my stomach to the top of my jeans. I almost stop breathing because every tiny touch is like a million small sparks igniting my body.

"You look so sexy lying there like that. It makes me want to fuck you in this chair."

"So do it," I challenge him, which is completely not me. It's like someone else has taken over my body.

He doesn't hesitate. Reaching for his shirt, he removes it in one smooth, quick motion.

I may have awoken the beast.

• • • ● • ● • • •

North

We pull up to the club where the bachelorette party is happening. My mom asked that Candy join them, and I tried to get her out of it, but Candy said she should participate. She also insisted I go to Jake's bachelor party.

So here we are several towns over at a club that doesn't look like the safest place for someone as sweet as innocent as my girl.

"I'm only down the road, so call me if you need me," I remind her for the tenth time.

"I promise I will, and if you decide you want to leave the bachelor party early, give me a call. I'll meet you out here, and we can both leave."

I give Candy a quick kiss and watch her head inside. When she gets to the door, she turns around and smiles at me, and all I want to do is jump out of the car and drag her back.

But I don't. I head to the bar, where I'm meeting Jake and his friends. I spot them off to the side, and my brother looks like he's having a good time. He's relaxed and smiling until his eyes lock with mine.

His smile drops, and he tenses. Guilt hits me because this is supposed to be his night, and I want him to have a good time. Is he feeling awkward about me being here? Maybe he feels forced into inviting me to his wedding.

I realize I don't care about the past anymore. I want Jake to be happy. I want him to be as happy as I am with Candy.

So I smile, walk up to my brother, and shake his hand. "I hope you and Vikki are happy together. I know I haven't said that before because I couldn't get past how you could betray me like that. But then I think of Candy, and if you and Vikki feel the same way I feel about her, then I understand."

My brother sags in relief. "Candy has been good for you, man."

"Yeah, she's been completely unexpected."

We started as a fake relationship. I don't know when it switched to something real, but in a short time, she's become someone I don't want to live without.

I plan to do everything in my power to get her to stay and show her how I feel about her. I plan to prove I'm not going anywhere.

Chapter 10

Candy

N orth said I didn't have to come to the bachelorette party tonight, but he suggested it would be a great way to bond with the other girls, especially since a few of his cousins were going to be here.

I feel so out of place. I've never been to a dance club before. I knew you were supposed to dress up, so I wore jeans and a nice shirt, but to say I'm overdressed would be an understatement.

Everyone at the bachelor party is wearing a teeny tiny dress that barely covers their butts with their boobs hanging out. They're in super high fuck me heels and wearing way too much makeup. They're also skinny as a rail, whereas I have plenty of curves.

Two of the women are married, one is getting married, and I know at least three of the others have boyfriends attending the bachelor party. I know bachelor parties are all about having fun, but I've never been to one like this.

I've been to a few clubs in college, but I don't remember them being this loud, dark, and packed. Clubs have never been my thing. The few times I went with a friend, I always left early.

I walk up to the bar to get a soda, and Vikki and a few of her friends are also standing there.

"Oh, look. There's North's new toy," Vikki says, and all the girls burst into giggles. "I don't know what he sees in you after having me."

"I don't cheat on him for one. And I'm not you, which is exactly why he likes me." I can't believe she still cares what her ex is doing when she's about to marry his brother.

My comments sober her up quickly, and she and her little group go off onto the dance floor. I sit at the bar and watch them. I've known girls like Vikki from school. She had North and didn't want him, but she sure as shit doesn't want anyone else to have him.

I figure it's probably best I stay away and let them do their thing. I can sit here for an hour or so while North spends time with his brother and family without worrying about me.

As my drink gets low, a man walks up to the bar beside me. "Can I get you another drink, sweetheart?"

"No, I think I'm okay, thank you." I try to be polite.

"What about a dance?" he tries again.

"I don't think my boyfriend would like that very much."

"Figures all the good ones are taken. I hope he knows how lucky he is." He winks, grabs his drink from the bartender, and walks off.

I check my email and social media on my phone, and after an hour or so, I look up to see what the girls are doing. My stomach turns at the sight that greets me.

The bride-to-be is making out with some guy who is not her fiancé. Her friends, who I know aren't single, are dancing all over some guys. It's not my scene, so I stay by the bar and wait until North is ready to pick me up.

A bit later, I text North to see how it's going on his end.

Me: How's the bachelor party?
North: Kind of lame for being the only sober one here. How are things going on your end?

I take a quick video of me sitting at the bar and show him my half-finished drink. I send it with the next text.

Me: Honestly, I'm pretty damn bored. This is not my scene.
North: You ready to leave?
Me: Only if you are.
North: Meet me out front in 15 minutes.
Me: See you soon.

I finish my drink, gather my purse, and head to the bathroom before I leave.

Even though a few girls are giggling and talking at the sinks, it's easy to hear two people having sex in one of the stalls. I do my business, but when I see the shoes of the woman in the next stall, I recognize them as the ones Vikki was wearing.

I finish and wash my hands, and a quick peek through the crack proves I'm right. There's no hiding that Vikki is blatantly cheating on her fiancé. Bachelorette party or not, cheating is cheating in my book.

I turn and leave the bathroom without looking back and make my way to the front of the building. North is pulling up as I step outside into the cool air.

By the time I get into his car, I'm pissed off at the whole situation.

Chapter 11

North

I can tell the moment Candy gets in the car that she's not herself. She seems pissed off and quiet, and I know something's wrong.

"Take me back to my place," she says when she closes the door.

Her voice is flat and cold. Not the bright, cheery person I've come to know over the last few days. I reach out and take her hand in mine. She lets me hold it, but she doesn't look at me.

"What's wrong?"

"Why did you insist I go tonight? Did you honestly think they'd welcome me with open arms?" she asks, the irritation clear in her voice.

"They weren't nice?" I quickly realize it's the stupidest question I could have asked.

"I don't remember a time when I've been treated so badly," she says as we pull into her driveway.

She wastes no time getting out and storming through her front door.

I sit there dumbfounded for a few seconds before I go after her. This is not the outcome I expected tonight. I thought we would have fun and funny stories about the bachelor and bachelorette parties. I reach her door and knock, thinking we'll talk this out.

"Go away. We'll talk about this tomorrow," she calls through the door.

And because I'll give her anything she wants, I turn and head back to my car, even though each step I take feels wrong.

• • • • ◆ • ◆ • • •

I don't sleep well. I keep thinking about what could've happened to upset my girl so much. I never expected her and Vikki to be best friends, but I thought she would at least have been civil to her last night.

I'm nervous as hell when I show up at her house this afternoon because we're supposed to be heading to the lake house for the reception and family dinner before the wedding.

When I get there, Candy is loading a suitcase into the back of her car. I pull in hesitantly and get out, unsure how this will go.

"I'm taking my car so I can leave if they behave like they did last night," Candy says, her voice cool and distant.

"Of course. Listen, I told my mom I wasn't happy with how they treated you, and she promised she'd handle it." After tossing and turning last night, I needed to do something.

"Great," she says, but I can hear the frustration in her voice. She looks at me like she has something else to say but decides against it. "Let's go. I'll follow you there."

She climbs into her car without another word. I need to find a way to fix this.

It's not a long drive to the lake house where the wedding is being held, and we're all staying tonight. With everything going on with Candy and me, it seems like a horrible time to be stuck in a house with my family.

We try to paste on a fake smile as we walk inside. When Jake sees us, he offers a big smile and nods in greeting. Vikki shoots Candy an evil glare.

Candy notices, and the smile falls from her face instantly. My mom steps over to them and says something that makes Vikki unhappy. Jake offers an apologetic smile.

My mother rushes over to our side. "Candy! North! We're so happy you're here. And I'm sorry about Vikki. I've said something to her, and she should be on her best behavior."

Before Mom gets a chance to say anymore, she's pulled away with a question from one of the staff.

"Yeah, because I'm sure that will end well," Candy mumbles before fixing the fake smile on her face again.

Chapter 12

North

We successfully avoid Jake and Vikki through the rest of the little get-together and rehearsal. I haven't left Candy's side. I don't know what's happened, but whatever it is, I'm not letting her face it alone.

At the reception dinner, our seats are close to the front, near Jake and Vikki's family. Vikki tried to place Candy at the other end of the table, but I put my foot down, and my mother agreed.

The dinner seems to go on and on and on. People give toasts to the couple left and right about how great they are, how cute they are together, and how well Jake treats Vikki.

Every time I look up, I find Vikki glaring at Candy, and my girl is uncomfortable. She's barely said a word or touched her food.

"North!" One of my brother's college buddies jumps up, grabbing my attention. "You've got to give a toast, man. You're the groom's brother!" He must be unaware of why I haven't been asked to give a toast.

"No, everyone else has this one covered." I try to brush it off with a smile, but some of his other college buddies jump in.

When I look at Vikki again, she's scowling at Candy, and so are a few of her friends. I squeeze Candy's hand and stand, and everyone quiets down. Vikki and Jake's eyes go wide, and Vikki gives a satisfied smirk like she's caught me in the act of having to speak nicely about her.

"I wasn't asked to give a toast tonight even though I'm the groom's brother. That's because when Vikki and Jake got together, Vikki and I were still dating." The room goes so quiet you could hear a pin drop.

Candy brushes my leg in silent support, and I smile at her.

"Vikki and I dated for a few years, and I thought things were great. I was ready to propose, and I had a ring in hand. Then I found her and my brother together. They'd been sneaking around behind my back for months rather than Vikki breaking up with me. It showed how much of a coward she truly is. I bet many of you are asking why I'm here at the wedding. Well, it's because my grandmother and my grandfather are here."

I look over at them and smile. My grandma has a huge smile on her face. I told them what happened between Vikki and me, and she said I should let her have it, so I know she's beyond thrilled that I'm finally standing up for myself. My grandfather has his gaze averted from Jake and Vikki—I'm sure he doesn't want them to know how he truly feels.

"I'm also here because my parents insisted. They wanted me to play the happy big brother role, and I tried. But now Vikki is treating my girlfriend like shit, and there's no excuse. Why should she care who I'm dating when she's marrying my brother?"

"Son, I think that's enough." My dad says calmly, trying to put an end to the situation.

"You're right. It is enough." I take Candy's hand, and she stands and follows me from the room. No one says a word the whole time.

The house has two wings, and the girls are staying on one side and the guys on the other. I wrap my arm around Candy's waist and lead her back to her bedroom.

"I bet that felt good, didn't it?" she asks as we head down the hallway.

"Yeah, it did. But I wouldn't have said any of it if she'd left you alone. Jake and I made amends last night. I hoped it was enough for all this to be over."

"Not for a girl like Vikki. She'll never be happy with anyone having you even though she didn't want you," Candy says, shaking her head as we reach her door.

She's talking to me, but I still feel the wall between us, and I want it gone. I want to get back to what we had before the bachelor and bachelorette parties. That easy-going girl whose smile lit up my entire world, I need her back.

Without thinking about it too much, I lean in and kiss her. I press her against the wall, wrap my hand in her hair, and kiss her deeply. My mouth dances on her, and she melts into me little by little.

When she wraps her arms around my waist, I feel that wall between us start to drop. I don't want to push my luck, so I reluctantly pull back from the kiss. But when I look at her face, it's soft, and she's smiling at me again.

"Get some sleep. It's a long day tomorrow, and you're going to be so sick of me at your side," I tell her, tucking a strand of hair behind her ear.

Candy nods and heads into her room.

Only once she closes the door behind her do I head back to my room on the other side of the house. I take the long way and go outside to get some fresh air, avoiding anyone who might be done with dinner.

Once back in my room, I start getting ready for bed when there's a knock at my door. I pray it's Candy coming to talk or spend the night with me and rush to open it without a second thought.

Chapter 13

Candy

As I get ready for bed, all I can think about is that kiss. I've been pretty upset at the whole situation, but during that kiss, I realized I shouldn't be upset at North.

The whole point of all of this was to make the wedding easier on him. The way he stood up for me at dinner is something I'll never forget. Outside of my dad, I've had no one stand up for me like that.

Being the curvy girl, I always found it easier to disappear into the shadows than make myself known. But I didn't mind having all eyes on me with North defending me.

I shouldn't be punishing North for the way Vikki's been acting. I shouldn't be making this week harder on him. I can only imagine what he's going through, even though he and his brother have made up.

I don't know if what we have has an expiration date, but I don't want to waste what little time I have left with him. So I pull sweatpants over my thin pajamas, check my hair and makeup and crack open my bedroom door.

I turn off my bedroom light and look around. I'm the only one out. I sneak down the hallway until I get to the main living area. A few people are relaxing in there, but I know I can cut through the kitchen to get to the wing where North's room is. He insisted on me knowing which room was his, and now I'm glad he did.

I casually walk toward the kitchen. "Can't sleep either, eh?" one of the guys says from the living room when he sees me.

"No, figured I'd come in and get something to drink before I head to bed," I tell him. He nods and turns back to whatever he has on the TV.

Once in the kitchen, I sneak into the hallway and down to the guy's side of the house. Thankfully, it's dark and quiet. I guess most people have retreated to their rooms.

I reach North's room and see the light under the door. I quietly open it, figuring I can sneak in, and we can talk. But the scene that greets me freezes me in my tracks.

Vikki is naked in the middle of his room, with a silk robe pooled at her feet. North is shirtless on the other side of the room, with his back pressed against the wall. When his eyes swing to me, they widen, and he looks like a kid caught stealing from the cookie jar. Vikki smirks at me, but they both remain silent.

So many thoughts race through my head, but there's one louder than the rest. I was a pawn in a game to get back at Vikki, to win her back for this moment right here. Why else would a sexy guy like North want to date the chubby nerdy librarian? He slept with me out of pity. I've experienced that one before.

"Thought a little payback for your brother was in order, huh? That's rich," I snap.

I turn without waiting to hear what either of them says and run back to my room.

"Candy! Wait!" North yells behind me.

Once in my room, I lock the door and put a chair in front of it.

"Candy! Please Listen!" North pounds on my door as I pack.

Once my bags are packed, I look around, thankful I'm on the first floor. I open my window and push my bag through, crawling out and running to my car. We were the last to arrive, so it's easy to get out of the parking area.

The first place North will look for me will be my place, so I head for my dad's.

Chapter 14

North

F uck. I don't think I've ever been so pissed in my life. The moment I cracked open my bedroom door, Vikki pushed her way inside. I put as much space as possible between us as she dropped her robe, and of course, that was the damn moment Candy walked in.

I can't blame her for running. By the time I turn and head down the hallway to the living room, everyone is gathered there, including Jake, Vikki, my parents, and my grandparents.

"What the actual fuck is wrong with you, Vikki? You're marrying my brother tomorrow, and you're still trying to hook up with me?" I yell, not caring that I'm raising my voice to a woman.

"That's not true. He came on to me," she whines to Jake.

"Really? How does that explain why you were naked, and I wasn't?" I snarl.

There's no way of redeeming this situation, not knowing how much Candy must be hurting.

I glare at my parents, who are standing off to the side. "Son or not, what just happened was beyond fucked up. But I'm glad to know whose side you stand on. Don't expect me at the wedding tomorrow or any other family event. I'm done."

I storm from the room and return to my bedroom, intent on packing and heading out to find my girl. Anyone who supports this marriage is no longer family to me.

I head directly to Candy's house, and even though I don't see her car out front, I get out and knock on the door, calling her name. The house is dark and quiet. She's not here.

Heading home, I pour myself a drink. I need to know she's okay, and I figure if she's not at home, she's with her dad. Her dad gave me his number the last time I saw him, so I shoot him a quick text.

Me: Is Candy there? I know she's mad, but I need to know she's okay.

So much time passes that I begin to think he's not going to message me back.

Bill Ellenson: She's here.

I stare at my phone, hoping he'll send me more, but he doesn't. I pour myself another drink and send Candy a text.

Me: This isn't over, and it's not what you think. Sweet dreams, beautiful.

I scroll up in our text message thread and watch the video she sent me from the bachelorette party. She was so bored, but I love the smile in her eyes when she's talking into the camera for me.

I watch the video on repeat a few times as I finish my drink. I'm about to close my phone when I notice something in the background. Vikki is all over another guy. He has her hand up her dress as they make out drunkenly on the dance floor.

I don't know her motive, but there's something else behind her marrying my brother. It's sure as hell not because she loves him. Not sure of my next move, I decide to call Ben.

"North? What's wrong?" he asks, answering on the first ring.

I glance at the clock. "Sorry, man. I didn't realize how late it was."

I tell him about the video Candy sent me at the bachelorette party and how everything blew up tonight.

"Damn, that was one hell of a dinner."

"Yeah, but I don't know what to do. Candy's not talking to me. I'm sure as hell not talking to my family, but I think this video should make its way to my brother."

"Your brother knows she's a cheater. She was cheating on you when they got together. I'm not sure it's going to make much of a difference. As for Candy, you need to give her time. You guys didn't have a conventional start, and she's probably doubting everything. Take a deep breath and give her some space to let her process. But don't give her too much space tomorrow. Pour your heart out to her, and don't leave anything on the table so you don't have any what-ifs."

We talk for a bit longer about how things are going with work with him before hanging up.

I get ready for bed and lie here thinking over everything Ben said. One phrase from my childhood plays on a loop in my head.

Always protect your family. And Carly is my family.

Chapter 15

Candy

I wake up at my dad's on Christmas Eve morning. I wasn't supposed to be here. North's brother is getting married today, but I'd rather be here with my dad and sister than at that wedding.

When I step into the kitchen, my dad and Parker are sitting at the table. I didn't tell them much other than I wouldn't be attending the wedding today and that I didn't want anything to do with North when I arrived last night. They respected my wishes, but I know they want the details.

I fix myself a plate and sit at the table, unsure where to start. I tell them how North and I started as a fake relationship, how we met at the diner, and the dates to get to know each other.

I gloss over us sleeping together, telling them about the bachelorette party, what happened last night at the dinner, and how North stood up for me. Finally, I talk about finding Vikki naked in his room and how I came straight here.

They listen to everything, only asking questions when they need something clarified. Once I'm done, Dad stands and pulls a bottle of whiskey from the top shelf of the cabinets, adding a dash to our coffee. He and Parker take a big gulp of coffee, but I don't think my nerves can handle it.

"I hate why you're here, but I'm happy to have some time with you. Let's get your mind North and start on the Christmas cookies," Dad suggests instead of making some big fatherly advice speech.

I guess he's onto something because we start making Christmas cookies, and before I know it, I'm laughing and smiling. My dad's phone goes off, and he steps away, leaving Parker and me to finish up.

After we've finished cookies, we start on our favorite Christmas movies, only to be interrupted by a knock at the door. Being the closest, I get up to answer it to see North standing on the porch steps.

I try to close the door on him, but he stops me. He doesn't miss a beat as he picks me up and tosses me over his shoulder.

"I've got her!" he yells as he closes the door behind us and heads to his truck.

"Put me down! What the hell are you doing?" I yell, kicking my legs and trying to loosen his grip.

It doesn't work, and North plonks me in his truck and buckles me up. I cross my arms and pout because my dad and sister aren't coming to help. He gets in, starts the engine, and heads to his place. Once we get there, I won't budge, so he unbuckles me and carries me inside.

He pauses to look at me. "Hear me out, and then if you want to leave, I'll take you home myself."

I glare at him for a long moment before finally nodding.

North releases a relieved breath. "When Vikki knocked on the door, I thought it was you. I was *hoping* it was you. She pushed her way in like I did to you just now. It's why I was on the other side of the room when she dropped her robe. I didn't touch her. She wasn't there more than ten seconds when you walked in."

"My yelling woke up everybody, and Vikki tried to spin quite a tale, making it look like I was trying to ruin the wedding. I went off on her and Jake. I told them I wouldn't be at the wedding, and I was done being part of the family. I went to your house, and you weren't there. I went home pissed and texted your dad to make sure you were okay," he explains, his words coming out in a rush.

"After texting you, I watched the video you sent me from the bachelorette party. In the background, you can see Vikki clearly cheating on Jake with some guy on the dance floor. I forwarded that video to my parents and Jake, and he's called off the wedding. He truly loved her and thought she'd be different with him. She told him she was pregnant, and he wanted to do the right thing. Of course, it was a lie. I messaged your dad, admitted everything, and told him I would make it right. That's the only reason he didn't stop me when I came for you. My parents have been begging for forgiveness, but none of it matters because I don't have you. I need you. I love you."

I gape at him. With those three simple words, he's stolen my breath.

Chapter 16

North

Candy doesn't say anything, so I continue talking.

"After the bachelor and bachelorette parties, I was going to ask you to be mine for real. No more games, no more fake relationship. This has been real for me from the beginning. What I feel for you is deep and strong. Stronger than anything I've ever felt. I love you, Candy."

I pull out the ring I've been carrying with me and drop to one knee. "I want to marry you, and I'll spend the rest of my life being worthy of you."

I look up at Candy, seeing the shock in her beautiful eyes.

"When I was texting with your dad, I talked to him about this. I have his blessing. Now, will you marry me, Candy Cane? Will you be my wife? Will you be my reason for getting up every day?"

"Yes," she says softly as my words finally sink in.

She holds out a shaky hand, and I slide the ring onto her finger. I could've done this at her dad's house, but I knew if I was going to propose, I wanted it to be here on the ranch.

I spend the rest of the day making love to my fiancée in every room in the house. We're up bright and early the next morning for Christmas Day and head over to her dad's.

When we walk into Bill's house, there's a huge smile on her face. Her dad and sister welcome me with open arms. It's like I'm instantly part of the family. I even sneak a few presents under the tree for them.

"Can we open gifts now?" Parker squeals like a little kid.

"Let's get some coffee, and then yes," Bill says.

I lean back on the sofa with an arm around my girl and watch them open their gifts. They're full of smiles and tease each other while laughing over memories of Christmases past. I can't wait to have kids and a family like this.

Parker jumps up, grabs a present, and brings it over to me. "This one is from Dad and me," she says, bouncing back to her place on the sofa.

I stare at them in shock. I wasn't expecting gifts from them. Bill and Parker have the biggest smiles as I open my present to find a beautifully detailed leather belt. It takes a moment to realize that my ranch name is engraved on the leather.

"This is beautiful," I say as I trace over the letters on the belt. "Thank you so much." I stand and give them both a hug.

"Okay, my turn. Keep in mind you weren't my fiancé when I bought this," Candy says, handing me another gift.

"Anything you get me would be perfect because you gave me you this year, and that's all I need," I tell her honestly.

This gift is bigger than the last one, and my hands shake a little as I open it. What I find is a saddle pad with my horse's name embroidered onto it.

"This is perfect, thank you." I lean in and kiss her in front of her dad and sister.

It's not a long kiss, but enough to show her what she means to me. When I pull away, she has a beautiful blush on her face.

"Now it's my turn." I get the presents I tucked at the back of the tree and hand one to each.

I got her sister a gift card to the arcade, where Candy said she likes to go and relax right by her school. I got her dad the belt buckle Candy said he'd love, and she was right.

All eyes turn to Candy when it's her turn. She smiles at me as she slowly opens her gift and gasps.

"Well, what is it? Don't keep us in suspense!" Parker bounces in her spot on the sofa.

"It's an old leather-bound copy of *Pride and Prejudice*," Candy says as she runs her hands over the cover of the book.

"It's not an original, but it's over a hundred years old."

Candy hugs me with tears in her eyes. "It's perfect."

After the gifts, the girls make hot chocolate and French toast bake for brunch, and we listen to Christmas music and talk. After brunch, I have one more surprise up my sleeve.

"Candy, I've got one more gift for you, but it was a little too big to get in the car, so it's at the ranch. I'm going to steal you away for a couple of hours, and we'll be back in time for dinner," I tell her, and a huge smile crosses her face. Her dad looks at me questioningly, and I wink. "I'm sure she'll send pictures. See you guys in a bit."

Candy is excited the entire way to the ranch, and as I pull in, I bypass the house and head straight for the barn.

"Okay, close your eyes," I tell her, placing a hand over them.

I lead her to the stall next to my horse and position her where I want her before removing my hand.

"Open them," I tell her. "I figured my fiancée needed her own horse on the ranch. This one is already saddle-trained. She's gentle and perfect for you. All she needs is a name and some love."

Candy squeals and wraps her arms around my neck, pulling me into one of the best hugs I've ever received. "I love her!"

Candy walks up to the horse and pets her, and they bond almost instantly. "Since I got her on Christmas and our names are Christmas-related, I think we should keep up the tradition. What do you think of Jingle Belle? And we'll call her Belle, for short."

Belle nods as if she can understand.

"I think it's perfect."

I've never been a huge fan of Christmas, but now I see its appeal. It's going to be our holiday.

Epilogue

Candy

Over a year later

Life couldn't be more perfect. North and I decided that even though Christmas was a massive part of our lives, we didn't want a Christmas wedding, so we got married that summer.

It was beautiful. Our color scheme was red and silver, we served candy canes, and we got married on the ranch so both of our horses could be involved. It was perfect.

North and his parents are still working on their relationship, as are he and Jake. All three were at our wedding, our biggest supporters outside my family.

North and I have spoken about it a lot, and he doesn't feel comfortable around his family like he used to. His brother apologizes every chance he gets. He thought he was in love, and when she told him she was pregnant, he wanted to do the right thing.

North and his brother hang out once a month, just the two of them. It's still a work in progress, but they're trying.

We've been to a few family dinners at his parent's place, and it's been awkward. I keep telling North they need to talk about the elephant in the room instead of ignoring it, but his mom always changes the subject when he tries to talk about what happened.

Since moving to North's ranch, I've never felt more at home. It's the place I was always meant to be. Moving out of the cottage that came with my job as head librarian allowed us to hire an assistant librarian, so now, I only have to work part-time. That means I get to do two things I love—working with books and working on our ranch.

It's the beginning of April, and things are starting to pick up for spring. We've enjoyed the slow downtime that comes with winter, and last month, North was dead set on getting me pregnant. He wants a Christmas baby so badly.

He would barely let me out of bed and was on a schedule of making sure I had enough of him in me to become pregnant. I'm not supposed to get my period for a few more days, but I took a test early because I felt off.

Sure enough, I'm pregnant. I called my dad and told him I had a surprise for North and needed him out of the house for a few hours today. So, Dad called him and asked for his help with something at his place. Of course, my husband jumped to help, giving me enough time to put together a neat little surprise for him.

I couldn't do too much without raising suspicions, but I headed into town to pick up a few items, including the cutest baby cowboy boots, Wranglers, and a flannel shirt. I have them all arranged on the dining room table around diapers and bottles, with my positive pregnancy tests front and center.

I even set up a spot for a hidden camera to get the whole moment on video. It was Parker's idea when she found out we were trying to have a baby so she could see his reaction.

Dad: He just left my place. Good luck!

I didn't tell my dad I was pregnant because I want North to be the first to know, but I'm sure he suspects. I can't wait to tell him and Parker. They're as excited for our family to grow as we are.

It takes about fifteen minutes to get from my dad's to our place. I pace the dining room until I hear the dog barking outside, indicating North's pulled up into the driveway. I take my spot at the back of the dining room so he'll have to walk past the table to get to me.

"Babe, I'm home. You better get naked!" he calls as the door closes behind him.

"I'm in the dining room," I call back, trying to keep my voice even.

"Perfect, because I'm ready to eat you," he growls and heads in my direction.

He enters the dining room, and his eyes land on me. He stops in his tracks because I can't take the huge smile off my face. Then he looks at the table and takes a few hesitant steps toward it.

I watch as he takes in everything on the table. He reaches out a shaky hand and picks up one of the pregnancy tests, the one that says positive in big letters.

When he finally looks up at me again, there are tears in his eyes. "Are you...?" He stops and brings his hand to his face, squeezing his eyes shut.

This man was emotional on our wedding day. He wasn't afraid for anyone to see he cried and all, but this takes the cake. He's even more emotional.

I walk up to him, place my hands on his shoulders, and wait for him to look at me again. "I am. I looked it up online, and my due date will be the week before Christmas."

A brilliant smile crosses his face as he bends and wraps his arms around my waist, picking me up and swinging me around in a circle.

"We have to call and tell everyone, and then I'm taking you upstairs and pampering you. You'll have no reason to leave your bed for the next nine months."

"Christ, North, I'll go stir crazy if I'm not allowed to leave the house, much less my bed."

"Fine, but you better start thinking of Christmas names because we're keeping the tradition going," he says as he pulls out his phone.

The first person he calls?

My dad.

• • • • ● • ● • • •

Want from the people of Walker Lake, Texas? Grab **The Cowboy and His Beauty!**

More Books by Kaci M. Rose

Rock Springs Texas Series

The Cowboy and His Runaway – Blaze and Riley

The Cowboy and His Best Friend – Sage and Colt

The Cowboy and His Obsession – Megan and Hunter

The Cowboy and His Sweetheart – Jason and Ella

The Cowboy and His Secret – Mac and Sarah

Rock Springs Weddings Novella

Rock Springs Box Set 1-5 + Bonus Content

Cowboys of Rock Springs

The Cowboy and His Mistletoe Kiss – Lilly and Mike

The Cowboy and His Valentine – Maggie and Nick

The Cowboy and His Vegas Wedding – Royce and Anna

The Cowboy and His Angel – Abby and Greg

The Cowboy and His Christmas Rockstar – Savannah and Ford

The Cowboy and His Billionaire – Brice and Kayla

Walker Lake, Texas

The Cowboy and His Beauty - Sky and Dash

Roping Her Curves

Taken By The Cowboy – North and Candy

Connect with Kaci M. Rose

Kaci M. Rose writes steamy small town cowboys. She also writes under Kaci Rose and there she writes wounded military heroes, giant mountain men, sexy rock stars, and even more there. Connect with her below!

Website

Facebook

Kaci Rose Reader's Facebook Group

Goodreads

Book Bub

Join Kaci M. Rose's VIP List (Newsletter)

About Kaci M Rose

Kaci M Rose writes cowboy, hot and steamy cowboys set in all town anywhere you can find a cowboy.

She enjoys horseback riding and attending a rodeo where is always looking for inspiration.

Kaci grew on a small farm/ranch in Florida where they raised cattle and an orange grove. She learned to ride a four-wheeler instead of a bike (and to this day still can't ride a bike) and was driving a tractor before she could drive a car.

Kaci prefers the country to the city to this day and is working to buy her own slice of land in the next year or two!
Kaci M Rose is the Cowboy Romance alter ego of Author Kaci Rose.

See all of Kaci Rose's Books here.

Please Leave a Review!

I love to hear from my readers! Please **head over to your favorite store and leave a review** of what you thought of this book!

Made in the USA
Columbia, SC
23 September 2024

42868556R00059